COOPER

A fish, a flower shop, a funeral home and a happy ending

BETH ZBASNIK

Illustrated by Gennel Marie Sollano

To order additional copies of this book, contact:
Xlibris
1-888-795-4274
www.Xlibris.com

Orders@Xlibris.com
ISBN: Softcover   978-1-7960-5525-2
           EBook   978-1-7960-5524-5

Print information available on the last page

Rev. date: 08/26/2019

There was once a sweet, little betta fish named Cooper. He had a wonderful life! Cooper lived in a shapely fishbowl, under the warmth of a big light, on a small table, in the middle of a flower shop. Every day, friendly customers stopped by to admire his pretty red tail and big, bright eyes as he nibbled on the roots of the peace lily that graced the top of his fishbowl.

One day the flower shop was very busy. People were scurrying everywhere. Cooper was a little troubled by the turmoil. All of a sudden, the flower deliveryman scooped Cooper's fishbowl off the table, carried it out the door, and stuffed Cooper into the back of the delivery van among many flower arrangements.

Oh no! What just happened? The van sped away. Cooper wondered, *Where am I going?*
Cooper sloshed around inside his bowl. He was so worried.

After many long minutes, the deliveryman finally stopped at a funeral home. Cooper had heard about funeral homes at the flower shop. He remembered hearing they are places where people gather to say goodbye to people who have died. He also remembered they are places where people gather to comfort one another when they are feeling sad.

All of a sudden, the van door slid open and the deliveryman began unloading the flower arrangements and carrying them into the funeral home. Then he picked up Cooper and carried him into the funeral home too!

It was very quiet inside, and Cooper was frightened.

Mr. Gotschall, the funeral home director, took Cooper from the deliveryman and placed him on a small table under a warm light.

Soft music was playing in the background. Some people were sitting in fancy chairs, and other people were standing in small groups talking to one another. Some people were just waiting in line to visit with their friends. Some people were sniffling, crying, and wiping their eyes. Other people didn't seem to be sad at all. Cooper wondered, *Am I at the calling hours for someone who died?*

Cooper remembered hearing about calling hours when people came into the shop and ordered flower arrangements for people who had died. Cooper was confused. He liked feeling the warmth from the light but really wanted to go back to his home in the flower shop. Mostly, he missed customers stopping by to visit him and admire his pretty red tail and big, bright eyes.

Suddenly, children in the room noticed Cooper! They looked just as confused and frightened as Cooper. But as they admired Cooper's pretty red tail and big, bright eyes, they began to smile and look happier.

Maybe Cooper could help children feel a little less frightened. Maybe he had found a new purpose. Maybe Cooper had found a new home!

Cooper began to feel more comfortable too! He liked seeing the smiles on the children's faces. He felt like his happy self again and no longer missed his flower shop quite as much. *Maybe*, he thought, *I should stay at the funeral home. Maybe there will be more children who want to visit with me and admire my pretty red tail and his big, bright eyes.*

Printed in the United States
By Bookmasters